W9-AAW-443

igloobooks

Written by Hannah Green
Illustrated by Sanja Rescek

Designed by Justine Ablett
Edited by Vicky Taylor

An imprint of Igloo Books Group,
part of Bonnier Books UK
bonnierbooks.co.uk

Published in 2019
by Igloo Books Ltd, Cottage Farm
Sywell, NN6 0BJ

Manufactured in China. GUA009 0519
10 9 8 7 6 5 4 3 2 1

Library of Congress Cataloging-in-Publication
Data is available upon request.

ISBN 978-1-83852-554-5
IglooBooks.com
bonnierbooks.co.uk

Love you more

I love you more than
jumping in rainy-day puddles. . .

. . . or splashing in a bath all filled up with bubbles.

I love you more than swimming in the sparkly sea. . .

. . . or having an adventure and climbing a tree.

I love you more than going on boats, planes, and trains. . .

. . . or zooming my race car around windy lanes.

I love you more than

ice cream on a hot, sunny day. . .

. . . or playing dress-up when
my friends come to play.

I love you more than
blowing out candles on a cake. . .

. . . or dancing to music with a

wiggle and

shake.

I love you more than

choosing toys from the shop. . .

. . . or you **tickling** my tummy until I beg you to stop.

I love you more than eating
a freshly baked apple pie. . .

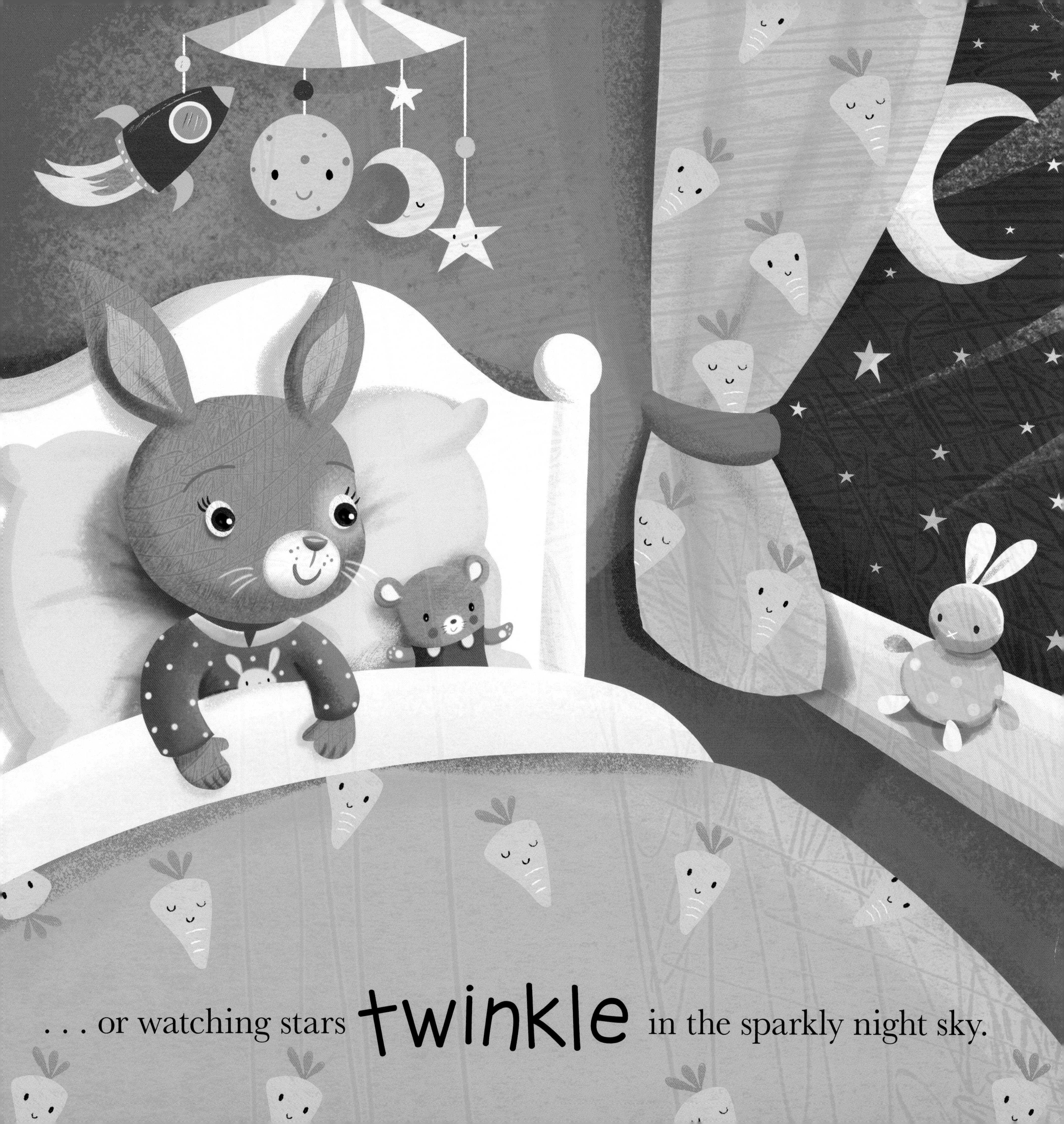

. . . or watching stars **twinkle** in the sparkly night sky.

I love you more than reading a book by the fire. . .

. . . or being pushed on the swings, going higher and higher.

I love you more
than building snowmen
in the snow,
or sledding down hills
to see how fast we can go.

I love you more than any of the things you do with me. . .

. . . because you are my fun,
caring, happy family.